Casper

THE FRIENDLY GHOST IN

GHOSTLAND

THIS WONDER® BOOK BELONGS TO—
_____

Casper
THE FRIENDLY GHOST IN
GHOSTLAND

Produced and Created by HARVEY CARTOON STUDIOS

Wonder Books®

PRICE STERN SLOAN, INC.

1987

CASPER, the friendly ghost, was not doing well in school. Instead of learning how to scare people, as he should have been doing, he sat and read fairy tales and daydreamed about how to make friends.

The three ghosts with whom he lived were worried about
his good behavior. He was no help at all around the house.
He was always oiling squeaky door hinges, polishing windows,
or sweeping away cobwebs. "How can any ghost haunt a tidy
house?" they wanted to know.

Worst of all, Casper would never join the other ghosts on scare raids. "It is very mean to want to scare people," Casper would say. "You should try to help people and make friends."

But the other ghosts would just laugh at him, and go out scaring people anyway.

One day the ghosts decided it was time to put a stop to Casper's good behavior. This was no way for a ghost to act. What was to be done? The ghosts put their heads together and decided to send Casper on a vacation. A trip to the Wild West would take his mind off good deeds and teach him to be rough and tough — like his cousin Spooky who was to go on the trip with him.

On the way to Tombstown, Casper and Spooky spotted a stagecoach. Spooky immediately set a bad example for Casper by scaring all the passengers and the driver. This made Spooky happy, but Casper was only sad.

They arrived in town just in time to see Bad Bart the Bully throw the sheriff into a watering trough. As the sheriff struggled to get out, the outlaw laughed loudly.

While the townspeople watched, Casper and Spooky wandered down the street. Casper said to himself, "The Wild West is even more unfriendly than home."

"They're not all unfriendly," said a voice behind them. "Just scared."

They turned around. There stood a little kitten whose name was Melody. "Why are they scared?" Casper asked her. "Are there bad ghosts out here, too?"

"No," she answered. "It's the rustlers. They've taken over the town."

"Can't the townspeople do anything?" asked Casper. Then he added, "I wish I could help."

"So do I," replied Melody. "Maybe we can. There's going to be a roundup tomorrow. The ranchers are trying to get all their horses together to keep the rustlers from stealing them. They can watch them better if they are all together."

"Good," said Casper. "Let's help them."

Bright and early the next morning, the roundup started. The cowboys from all the ranches herded their horses together. As they approached the main corral, Casper tried to help by running to open the gate.

But it might have been better if Casper had not tried to help at all!

"A ghost!" the cowboys shouted.

At this, the horses broke away and stampeded across the plain. The cowboys scattered in all directions.

Grabbing their guns, Bart and his gang rounded up all the horses and drove them to their secret hideout in a canyon.

Casper and Melody convinced Spooky to help them find the horses. On the way, they met Nightmare, the ghost horse.

"Hello, Casper," said Nightmare. "I thought I'd fly out and join you on your vacation."

"You're just in time," said Casper. "We need your help to find some stolen horses."

Finally, they discovered the canyon. Casper told his friends of his plan. "Nightmare," he said, "you will lead the horses to safety while Spooky and I catch the attention of the rustlers."

Casper drifted over to the boulder behind the outlaws' campfire. "I am your conscience," he moaned in a low, low voice. "You are bad. You should not steal!"

At this the bandits trembled and shook. They never noticed that the horses they had stolen were trotting quietly out of the canyon.

"Casper is taking too much time!" thought Spooky. "I'll fix these outlaws!" With that he made himself visible and screamed, "BOO-O-O-O!!!" at the top of his lungs.

"A ghost!" yelled the outlaws. They got up and started to run.

"No!" shouted Casper, jumping out from behind the rock. "We won't hurt you." But the rustlers had already fled.

"Well," said Casper, "at least the horses are safe. But now we'll never be able to capture the outlaws or make them good."

When Casper, Melody, Spooky and Nightmare reached the town, however, they were in for a surprise. The rustlers had already been there and demanded that the sheriff lock them up in jail to protect them from the ghosts!

When Melody explained to the townspeople that Casper was really a friendly ghost and had brought back their horses, they immediately made him an honorary deputy sheriff and gave him a bright shiny badge to wear on his chest.